I0639968

Arthur Edward Waite

Lucasta, Parables and Poems

Arthur Edward Waite

Lucasta, Parables and Poems

ISBN/EAN: 9783744729345

Printed in Europe, USA, Canada, Australia, Japan

Cover: Foto ©Andreas Hilbeck / pixelio.de

More available books at **www.hansebooks.com**

Lucasta

PARABLES AND POEMS

BY

ARTHUR EDWARD WAITE

"I see the better things of the life to come before mine eyes."
A New Light of Alchymy.

LONDON
JAMES ELLIOTT & CO.
TEMPLE CHAMBERS, FALCON COURT, FLEET STREET, E.C.
1894

TO MY WIFE.

CONTENTS.

With Harp and Crown.

SONS of the Morning and Eternity,
    Children of Benediction and of Light,
Daughters of angels' kisses, I have wrought
A little book of melody and love —
A book against the Resurrection Day,
Song-mystic of humanity divine,
Achieved in one regenerated youth,
Our bright, sidereal beacon — Israfel.
I swear, my brethren, by the Orphic faith,
And by the faithful prophecies inscribed
Deep in discerning souls, that starry hosts,
Empyrean kings, and galaxies of gods,
Lead on that Spirit, and his reign is nigh.
He stands erect among frankincense clouds,
A pillar of melody.   His saffron hair
Is a cloud of harpstrings : as he moves in grace
And ministers, the ground beneath his feet
Quivers in music like a sounding-board ;
The parted air about him slowly streams

Into faint flute-notes.   In God's Holy Place
He wears himself the aspect of a God :—
Has eyes, and sees celestial hierarchies,
And companies of martyrs and of saints,
Who from the four-square basis of the Church,
Now visible and militant on earth,
Slope off, ascending to the apex point
Whence undimensional Deity looks down
O'er the vast triangle of intelligence,
Upreaching towards beatitude and light :—
Has lips which shape man's language to divine
By inspiration of divinity,
And voice it past the common range of sound,
To traverse God's infinity as prayer :—
Has ears wherein celestial melodies
Find passage to the galleries of soul,
Wherein they circulate and amplify,
As in white sea-shells tinged with coral pink
All ocean's vastness hollowly resounds :—
Has hands to sanctify by service meet,
Among the vessels and the mysteries :—
Has feet ascending to the Throne of God :—
And, with a clamorous music in his throat,
Utters the watchwords of Eternity.

Sons of the Voice and Peers of Everlasting,
Monarchs of organ-melodies, against

The meeting of the Bridegroom and the Bride,
I bring you once again a little book
Of transformation on the psychic plane—
Most magical, miraculous, emprize,
Which by imagination's power intent,
Was truthfully accomplish'd and endures.
O may Lucasta's litanies and chants,
This praise of love, this praise of maiden light,
These visionary parables and songs,
This hidden meaning, this arcane romance,
Be counted as the prophecy and pledge
Of more resplendent exploits still to come—
The transmutations of your Orphic art !
I look to see most mighty things of God,
Accomplish'd in the land of living men !
The unprepared but pure hypostasis
Developed and elaborated here,
Was one fair-shining maid's simplicity ;
She in her outward, manifested life,
Remains beside me as a gracious sign,
A sacramental type of hidden truth,
Reality, and beauty, which transcend
Expression.   We are born with faces veil'd
As Moses' was, to hide the God within—
Lucasta's mystic veil with Horeb's light
Is now transfigured, Earth and Heaven are join'd
In an alchemic marriage, which transmutes

The world to gold.   Discriminate between
The letter and the spirit that informs—
Be, then, lucidity and lustre yours,
Peace, inspiration, pure imagining,
Unspotted spirit in a frame unsoil'd,
A royal robe, a grand and dreadful doom,
A mission, a revealment, a wide sea,
An open sea, a boat to sail thereon,
Laurel, and sacred palm, and Crown of Life !

Prologue.

I.

IMAGINATION, clothing mortal form
  With attributes of Deity, be thou
My minister! Immortal Will, proclaim
Thy strength once more! Magician of the mind,
Directing both, divine, eternal soul
Of inspiration and of poesy,
Thy high, creative faculties assume,
Thy concentrated energies collect,
For holy task! On thee the mantle falls,
It wraps thee round in vivifying folds—
Though o'er thee broods an unresponsive sky,
And round thee spreads a disillusion'd world,
Mind can illumine both, begin thy spells.
A life is put into thy priestly hands
To beautify, develop, and inform—
To lead by evolution of the mind,
From realm to realm of ideality.

Creative frenzy searches all my soul ;
The panorama of the outward world,
Before mine eyes transfigured in a breath,
Is supernaturally glorified.
The inspiration lights up earth and sky,
And some far-gleaming pageantry, some flash
Of crumbling crests proclaim the open sea,
Mine adoration and my heritage.
O one thing more to beautify and bless —
One human soul to deify —one maid
To drape with immortality--one deep,
Illuminating, infinite dream of love !

High art and duty call, for whatsoe'er
Imagination, by its lofty spells,
Confers on beautiful and human things,
May well, projected by a conscious mind,
Become the chosen object's attributes,
However much it be invisible ;
May even by effort of determined will,
A plastic, passive, nature permeate,
Until imagined beauty, glory, grace,
Shine realised and visible therein
With eminent perfection.   Be it thus—
Be this imagination's holy end !
For no transmutatory enterprise
Transcends love's grand, illimitable range,

Who, after every possible emprize,
Retains profound, potential energies
For new achievements on the golden lines
Of that ineffable, surpassing art
And splendid path of ideality,
Which in the order of the intellect
Lifts glorified humanity to God.

II.

The supplicated power of poesy,
Imagination's high, creative aid
Have beautified thine incarnation fair,
Of modest, maidenlike humanity.
The strength implored in turn from Heaven and'Earth,
Sky's brightness of deep azure swooning off
To softest lilac on the misty verge ;
The sea's invigorating influence,
The airy ecstasy of open downs,
Wind-swept, and flooded by a midnight moon,
The concentrated faculty of will,
And inspirations, caught at intervals,
From infinite, imperial realms of thought,
Have each and all in many a mystic mood
Their solemn part of ministry perform'd ;
But all dependence on the outward world—
This summer spectacle of mead and wood,

Of early moon which buoys a phantom shell
In ether's shining depths—seems needless now.
Thy rosebud grace, before the magic glance
Of sympathetic contemplation, bursts,
With sudden plenitude of loveliness,
Into a perfect flower, whose affluent bloom
Attracts the venerating sense of art ;
Whose fragrance trances thought ; attraction turns
To passion, passing as an incense up,
And leaving crystal gold of perfect love
Upon the holy altar of the heart
Fire-tried and shining.   Veil on veil removes,
And then the wonder of a lambent star
Above the gracious presence of thy brow,
Doth in a solemn and a metric trance
Of silence meet and worshipful begin
To manifest a majesty of light
And gentle radiation.   Five at length
Complete the lucent chaplet ; then I see
Thy nature's heights withdrawn and cryptic depths ;
The circular progression of thy soul
Reveals its phases, all its latent strength,
Its unelicited abilities
For dread achievement.   Thou art infinite ;
The unform'd vastness of thy beauty, strength,
And thine unlimited capacities
For life, love, truth, have taken partial shape

And faint expression in thy mortal form,
Where maiden elegance and charm of mien
Hint dimly the Invisible within.
I will not say that thine is vaster strength,
Thy spiritual beauty's vistas more
Prolong'd, thine altitude unsearchable
Beyond all height, depth more profoundly sunk,
And striking roots of being in the dark
Abyss of God, more infinitely low
Than other souls.   There are unfathom'd depths,
Untravell'd spaces, undetermined heights
In every heart.   There is no human soul
Whose possibilities can be limited ;
Whose utmost point of progress can be mark'd
On any chart ; but most are veil'd to me.
Thine opens slowly, as the ether bares
Its shining distance through the parted clouds,
After a storm, at evening.   I am bound
By that divine revealment evermore
Thy being to develop and expand.

III.

Invoked with passion of a purpose fix'd,
That potent Monad which in life o'erbroods
The psychal man, directing searching light,
Has rectified and clarified and cleansed

The chemical florescence of the soul,
And gross purgations of man's coarser part.
O trustfully resign thy gentle self,
And I will bear thee hence to holy hills
Of noble intellectuality !
From all things common. limited, and low,
To all things lofty. limitless. and rare,
To naked peaks above the line of snow,
The mountains of the mind, the breathless, free,
Capacious world of visionary thought—
Beyond ambition of the boldest lark,
Beyond the eagle's flight—a realm unknown—
An unexplored, intelligible realm,
Invested with the majesty of dream.—
There is no peace, no beauty in the glare
About these low, relaxing meadow-lands.

I bless Thee for the bracing mountain-air
Which freshens all the summits of the Soul,
Thou mighty God !   I yearn—I yearn—to Thee !
My heart ascends in aspiration pure
To meet Thy majesty and tranquil light ;
Another being in my arms I bear—
Baptise her beauty in benignant beams,
Invest her with the liberty complete
Of Thine illuminated and elect !

Parables.

The First Parable

THE GENERATION OF LUCASTA.

THE generations of immortal soul,
   High soul in delicate and dainty form
Of marvellous mortality! . . .
                There floats
A pungent perfume, changing every step
And sweet in each mutation. Does it come
From orchards nigh me, from the garden close,
Or clover meadows? . . . 'Tis the evening breath
Of nature lapsing towards her night's repose,
In bridal splendour of the latest spring
Right royally invested. How my life
Expands within it, and is bathed therein!—
Deep, deep it drinks!
              What golden gates unbar!
What cryptic springs of melody unseal!
I float serenely up life's lucent stream
Into the further past. I see thy soul

Serenely dwelling in its fontal home—
In spiritual mansion bright and blest —
Thine ante-natal state—a virgin clime,
A purple plain of unalloy'd delights,
Twelve cubits sphered above the loftiest hills,
The phœnix-home of immortality,
And morning joy.   The golden rule of life,
From star to star its undisputed sway
Immutably extending, has evolved
From out the simple, pure, subjective state,
By an interior, harmonious law,
A portion of thy nature into form.
The inner essence takes an outward shape
Of melody made visible, conform'd
To that divine and individual thought
Eternal cause had consciously express'd
To bring thee into being. . . . Is it well
To call thee fair, to say thy mien is high,
Thy vesture argent, and thy lily crown
A star-eclipsing wreath of loveliness?
I see thy perfect, superhuman form,
Like poetry in happy music clothed,
But thine unsearchable, unbounded soul
Has human shape alone to human thought.
I sense thy presence in the sphere of mind,
I know not what thou art ; I call on thee,
And thou respondest in the brightest shape

Supreme imagination pictures, based
On human form.   I see thy haunting eyes,
Like evening's grey from Heaven's eternal hills
View'd in a holy trance.   I pass therein—
Through fragrant spaces, poised on eager wings
Of upward aspiration—pass in dream ;
I see thy timeless origin express'd
In spiritual symbols—a pure spark
Or point of life intense, profoundly plunged
In the electric ocean of God's bright,
Essential intellectuality.   .   .   .   .
Support the dreamer now, ye mighty downs,
Thou scarlet sunset, draped in formless cloud,
Pinewoods, and wilderness, and windy peaks,
And shadow-haunted prospects far prolong'd,
And closing night ! . . . An inner impulse prompts
That point of light ; above the burning sea
It lifts itself ; a radiant globe it grows,
And down creation's stream of forming life
It glimmers slowly into consciousness.
The conscious life consumes the shining form ;
It turns one thought intent ; through ages long
It feeds upon itself, and, sinking far,
Its own unsearchable profundities,
And unimaginable, endless heights,
It dimly measures, till the vast beyond,
The contact form'd with God at either end,

Pulse and vibrate therein ; the tide of thought
Turns outward then ; sense-music charms it on,
Desire and will unite ; the magic change,
Encompass'd enigmatically, gives
The outward shape.   Thou takest angel form,
And in the sexless, simple world of soul—
The purple plain of unalloy'd delights
Diaphanously draped, with wide, white wings.
One torch-like star, from pale and lofty brow
Diffusing light—and auburn hair unbound
In rainbow ripples— thus I picture thee.

Still works the outward evolution's law,
And towards the circle of material things
It draws thy nature out.   A vortex takes
The circle ever towards its central depths,
And downward sailing with the mighty tide.
Eyes fixed for ever on eternal things,
Thou enterest the generating world
A narrow passage with a door of night
At either end, a golden hope beyond,
Cross, combat, victory, and crown betwixt.

The generations of immortal soul,
High soul in delicate and dainty form
Of marvellous mortality !

The Interlude.

In Exile.

THE town recedes, the turbid stream is cross'd ;
  The heart that throbs beneath the weight of worlds
Is borne with no more stress of steaming steeds
Than this child-heart beside me. . . .
                   Queen of Stars,
White-breasted Virgin, tender, trusting, true,
Translucent Lily, pour thy dainty light—
White light, bright fragrance, beautifying earth,
Whose shadows melt in parabolic morn
Of maiden mildness and enravishment,
While every desert place thy being's pure,
Intelligible harmonies invest
With lily blossoms in thy likeness made,
All lustre, softness ! . . . . Now the leaning elms
Line country lanes, which take through gentle scenes—
May-scented still, their dilatory way ;
Now burning sunshine floods transforming skies,
And winds are winsome as the voice of Christ

In childhood wafted over Syrian fields ;
Now pleasant pools, with basking swans beside,
In dim recesses spread their brown expanse.
And something ever of exalting light,
Which thine eyes lend to all on earth and sea,
Has visibly transfigured and enrich'd
Those golden slopes of uplands far away.
Thy consecrated, delicate, gentle lips,
The homes of spiritual melody,
On thy true poet's still in trance are press'd :
Thy warm arms clasp him, thine eyes shine on him ;
And when the amplitude of all the world,
With woodland wastes and miles of dreaming fell,
And an intolerable, seraphic sky,
With sudden rushing of awaken'd wind
From buoyant seas, invigorates once more
The sacrificing priest of Nature's shrine,
And breaks up every fountain of the soul
Into floods of adoration—then I know—
Yon naked heath, with heaven drawn out beyond,
A threshold of the infinite, assures ;
That one black pine upon the dizzy hill,
And orchard-closes' plenteous prophecies,
This sacred and illuminating truth
Do visibly and sensibly infuse—
That thou, sweet maid, though meek in all thy ways,
And not more firmly poised on breathless heights

Of unattainable virginity,
And dread Uranian loveliness, than low
Immersed in glad humility of thought,
And parted far from vanity as I
From thy pure peace aud haunting sanctity,
Art truly Queen of Stars, Christ-lighted moon
Of soul-effulgence, shedding mystic rays,
And sprinkling melody of countless larks
Entranced in morning ether. Do I err?
Let cold imaginations bound to sense
Misread thy beauty's parable profound,
No less that Cosmos of incarnate soul
Shall in the incandescent light of love—
Before the quicken'd faculties of mind—
Burn gorgeous, golden.
     Whether love reveals
Pure love that clarifies and purges sight—
Or by its spiritual chemistry
Transmutes, transfigures, still the change is true.
Thine outward beauty is a hand which points,
Which leads by lily-lined, azalean paths
To the seraphic and ineffable shrine
Of thy soft, shining, thine unsullied soul.
The outward charm that binds a thousand hearts
Is but the shadow of thy loveliness,
The first faint fragrance of the full-blown rose
Inhaled from far, a promise of the deep

Intoxication of ecstatic sense,
When venerating hands shall part its screen
Of jealous leaves, and bent. adoring face
Press lips against its petals.

The Second Parable.

A Golden Key to a Mystic Palace.

A CRYSTAL palace, built by mortal hands,
Uplifts the splendours of its tetrad form,
Above the level pastures, on the height :
A crystal cresset to a world of dreams,
It stands transfigured. As the sinking sun
Invests all commonplace and humble things
With poetry and glory, this light pile,
By mortals built, by mighty genii plann'd,
Is draped for ever with a rainbow sheen,
And from diaphanous and hyaline.
Through opal transits, to refulgent turns,
And scintillates and coruscates, and shines
With countless vivid and prismatic hues,
While every Gilead breeze that breathes around
Is raised by passage of angelic wings, —
For there Lucasta dwelt. Her steps therein
Awoke adoring echoes. There her voice
Did, thrush-like, stir in the enravish'd air

Vibrations subtly circulating still,
And stirring timelong in the hearer's mind
The pulse of purest thought.   In secret nooks,
In sacred chambers utterly apart,
By fountain sides, by many a spellbound lake,
By solemn statues, still her voice is stored.
In tiny ripples of ecstatic song
Is audible at times to ears elect.
She haunts them still—the palace and the park—
As those pale spiritual clouds of gold
Are by the vanish'd sunbeams haunted still.

Thou crystal cresset to a world of dreams,
I enter thee, thy haunted halls explore !
I know thee well, I dwelt myself in thee,
But darkness reign'd, and spurr'd by powers without,
I scaled thine endless flights of hollow stairs
To ghostly turrets with a soul adread
And nameless doom above.   Now light has dawn'd,
And from thy windows on the age to come,
By prophesy and parable and dream
Made evident, by all our hopes ensured,
The mystic thinker looks.   Creative thought
Has limn'd its landscapes, it is nigh this day,
It passes all our schemes—it comes, it comes !

O solemn Night, involving earth and sea !
With inspiration my receptive soul

By all its channels of perception fill !
Thy May-time fragrance, like a wine, exalts,
Thy cool wind wraps imagination round,
And lifts it into prophecy.   Thy dews
Refresh, thy darkness haunts, thy stars untold—
O Night, the joyful wonder of thy stars !—
Prostrate my spirit in adoring love !
Ah, mystic, tender, mild, maternal Night,
With silent tides of shadow lap me round !
Ah, haunting lavender of fusing sky !
Ah, fading saffron, atmospheric grey—
Clear as Lucasta's eyes !   Eternal speech,
Among the tops of tall and trembling trees,
Prolong your parables and mysteries !
O magic space of sleep and dream and love,
Beneath thy sleepless trees, thy brooding sky,
I utterly adore thee !   On these downs,
By mighty spectacles of open sea
In stormy moods of majesty—in all
Thy moods and phases, wheresoe'er thou art—
I praise thee, minister to me thy scald !
I place my spirit in thy holy hands—
Haunt, thrill me, fill me, thy desire and love
Make agony of illimitable void,
Which frenzied inspiration pouring forth
Alone can soothe, which thou alone canst fill,
Until the rosy morning of my soul,

Lucasta, come, with light of liquid eyes
And stream of aureate tresses-- honey-lipp'd,
Dew-fed, sea-scented, and syringa-crown'd.
Fall dimly, then, serene and holy Night,
And let the tender marvel of her eyes
Thy dusk and mournful spaces glorify !
Fall softly, then, most cool, enchanted Night,
And let the pulses of Lucasta's heart
With secret words enrich thy mystery !
O bend thy beautiful and star-crown'd head,
Hush all thy winds, and lull thy latest bird.
And let the melody of Lucasta's voice
Upon the tideless surface of thy soul's
Unfathomable ocean wake some light
And silver ripples, from whose tender gleam
Shall rise the crescent of a new-born moon
To beautify thy being !

The Interlude.

THE MESSAGE.

MY Star has shed one beam of purest light
    To soothe me by lone waters wandering,
My Swan one feather in her starry flight
     Has shaken from her wing,
Vibrating with melodious delight ;
And with the voice of seraphs, when they sing
  Their unknown canticles ineffable,
     My virgin Philomel,
My Dove that, dwelling in Dodonian grove,
  On dread, divine, immutable decrees
     Of all providing Fates,
Amidst the rustle of Æonian trees
     Vaticinates,
Hath sung me one revivifying song
  Which lifts me straight from darkness into day—
A thousand echoes in my soul prolong
     The silver lay ;
It cools all fever, as a fountain's spray

Makes cool the forehead on an August day ;
    Again my heart is strong,
My toiling brain intuitively clear :
    Mine eyes behold reality and truth ;
The harmonies of every starry sphere—
Endow'd with inner faculties—I hear ;
That golden and unconquerable youth—
        Pure, buoyant, and divine,
Which under some more favour'd influence
Than common stars of destiny dispense,
        Had once been mine—
That youth flows bounding now through every vein ;
I hold the measure of the mighty main
    Within the single compass of my being ;
The bounds of possibility expand,
    There is no scheme too grand,
        No doom too great for dreeing.
And throned for ever on the seat of mind—
All doubts dispell'd, all darkness left behind—
Divine imagination, purged from Earth,
        Beholds the world's new birth—
Beholds the future, like a formless sea,
Stretch, ever bright'ning, to infinity,
    The evolution into dream'd Ideal
        Of that we call the Real,
And through the purple vistas of the distance.
The Magic and the Meaning of Existence !

The Third Parable.

THE MANIFESTATION OF LUCASTA.

ALL sense of duty seems in thee to merge,
    I have no duty left but love for thee ;
I have no hopes, no dreams, no conscious thought ;
I do not breathe nor feel, I am no more,
I simply love, I "love but live no more."
The passion in me, like a radiant star,
Through all the world in light and warmth diffused,
Embraces all, contains and searches all.
I love the world in thee, serve man in thee.
I worship all things beautiful in life
When my pent spirit its existence pours
In ardour forth on thee.   O love, love, love !
O adoration of ecstatic love,
The entrance to the palace of the King,
Against all scorners closed and barr'd and seal'd,
With twelve hermetical and mystic seals !
O Salem, city on the mountain-top !
O promised land of honey and of milk !

O Aden, Eden, land of holy dream !
O House of God !   'Tis cold to call thee strong,
'Tis weak to call thee beautiful, 'tis vain,
With the drear commonplace of mortal speech,
To name thy storms, thy calms, thy heights, thy depths
To call thee joy, to call thee life of life,
For thou art love, which names both man and God—
Which names creation's law, whose fourfold term
Is God's own mystic city built four-square,
The everlasting, mighty tetragram.
Thou art salvation, immortality,
The resurrection and the crown to come:
Thou art God infinite, thou boundest all :
Darkness and horror and the deep abyss,
The void and vortex of impurity,
Chaotic malice, arrogance, and hate—
Those deaths in life—alone devoid of thee.

'Tis not the moon whose spiritual light
Has spell'd the sea, for thou art moon and sun
And in immeasurable ocean thou
Assumest other majesty and form :
Thy grace is in acacia and in beech,
And when thy lover in a lane at noon
Beneath some maple lays his languid limbs,
And those broad, beautiful, benignant leaves
Make shade and shelter in a torrid time,

And drooping low with lissome whispering
Fan fever'd forehead and in ears adream
Recite dryadic rhymes and roundelays,
It is the providence of thy pure love
Which closes round him ; on thy lap he lies,
Thy heart the moss which pillows, and thy breath
The zephyr, the leaf-messages thy voice,
And those dryadic rhymes and roundelays—
The rhythmic efflorescence of thy soul,
Whose depths are resonant with organ-odes
And the high epics of eternity.

A haunted house where ghosts and mortals dwell
Together, in a city of the dead—
The dreadful city of the dead in soul—
I, bent on secrets to be won from death,
Ambitious of the dream'd-of life beyond,
And ardently, incessantly devour'd
With aspiration to prolong life's line
Round all the circle of eternity,
Sought out, won entrance, took my place assign'd,
Among the hush'd and necromantic throng,
And round a table such as Merlin plann'd,
We communed nightly with the men call'd dead.

Ye melancholy shadows of the past,
Ye unsubstantial entities, ye thin

Phantasmata, reflecting back my thoughts-
With dim, repellent, unobservant eyes,
And baleful blue and phosphorescent lights—
About the darksome chamber floating slowly
In ominous silence—was it there and then,
On such an awesome and forbidden quest,
That any light native to earth or sea
Could ever reach? . . . A sacramental pause
Came in that thaumaturgic mystery,
And with the brightness of thy human laugh,
And with thy human presence passing fair,
Thou didst its space enrich and beautify.

I sought the wither'd leaves of fairy gold,
And I found thee, a true and living wealth,
The vivifying seed of deathless gold,
Within the ivory casket of thy fresh,
Intelligible beauty. . . . Not at once—
O many moons of misery and want,
Of passion spent in vain, of lines misread
Through all the tangled skein of destiny,
Of inspiration round the idol-shrine
Long squander'd in abortive prophecy.
The harvest moon of fruit and fulness shines-
The skein unrolls, the knots are loosed therein.
The inspiration finds an impulse new,
The prophecies discredited assume

A new significance and solemnity ;
For by the psychic telegraph of thoughts,
From mind to mind incessantly transferr'd,
Thou dost electrify me day by day
With beautiful imaginings, with soft
And tender messages, with odours sweet
Which ever follow upon fancy's flight,
Uprising, bird-like, from thy being's nest
With random lines of poetry, song-bursts,
Sky-fallen cadences. I stand this day,
As in the middle of a mighty wold
Which open heaven enrings, still belted round
By normal sequences of circumstance
In common and unvisionary spheres ;
But on the verge an arch of rainbow light—
With battlemented turrets of pure gold,
With blazon'd banners of the sunset land—
Star-glister'd—edified by elfin kings
And powers pontifical of fairyland—
In shining stillness stands the entrance-gate,
Gate Beautiful, to thine own nature's world.
My path is there ; it leads from mundane things,
'Tis lost in thee—from disenchantment thou
The refuge, all things common and unclean,
O exaltation, poetry, and joy !
The bright illimitable elfin land
Of thy regenerating beauty's depths—

My path is there, my path, O soul ! is there,
And there romance shall lead through all my life
By mead and stream, o'er uplands cool and high,
Through harvest fields, exploring further still,
Sense-thrilled, enraptured, borne on ardent wings,
Thy woman-world.   And gazing backward thence
That haunted house, where ghosts and mortals dwell
Together in a city of the dead,
Becomes itself the mystic rainbow arch,
The portal of the palace of the queen ;
The phosphorescent vapours brooding there
Are blazon'd banners of the sunset land ;
And those dim ghosts with unobservant eyes,
And cold corpse-touches, are the elfin hosts,
Which on the threshold of the elfin world
Seem spectres, ever to the dreamers sunk
In drear delusions of Reality.

The Interlude.

THE wind blows freshly. In this morning light
  The beauty round should win discerning praise,
But through the threshold of thy glorious eyes,
By magical election, have I gazed,
And I have seen thy soul. All stars, all seas,
Are stripped of beauty now . . . .
      O mighty main,
Lift thine immeasurable voices high !
Stars of the distant twilight, circle still—
Reproach me all, and chide thy chosen priest,
Sweet Mother Nature ! I adore thee still,
Most wondrous world of waters ; thy bright breast,
At once placidity and restlessness,
All light, all azure—like Lucasta's face—
Is but an efflorescence of thyself,
Thy grandeur, depth, and mystery. Her height,
Her soul's unconscious height of chastity ;
Thy depth, thy vastness, seem but phases all
Of one unsearchable secret.
      Her I see,

Who distant in the City of the Blest,
Will tarry in cool shadow till I come,
When, in the vigour of the morning wind
I stand, self-poised, upon a peak of rock,
And all thy glittering and gladsome pomp
Of hasty tide about me swirls and swells :
While every shallow in the shingly shore
Is like a boy's voice meeting careful life
With blithesome laughter —all the distant depth
Speaks as with tidings of a mission'd man,
Who from the heart and centre of all things
Ascends with revelation.   Thou art there,
When in the dreadful City of the Blest—
The dreadful City by thy beauty Blest—
I stand absorb'd in adoration deep
Before Lucasta's eyes.   Absorb'd I stand !
Grey eyes—Madonna—adoration deep—
Immeasurable main of mighty soul—
Seraphic spirit—thou hast fill'd the world !
There is no sea, no sky, no fertile earth ;
'Tis not the lark which sings, the summer wind
That cools and freshens ; it is thou in each—
Thou variously, inscrutably reveal'd,
And plunged for ever in a dream of thee—
My soul no more a separable form—
I lose myself, I melt, I merge in thee ;
For in the circle of all knowable things

Thou only art reality and truth,
Though mystic voices, which are part of thee,
Vibrating oft the visionary air,
Divide the hush intent of ecstacy
With names—the images of things unknown--
With high prophetic names—thy Christ, thy God !

The Fourth Parable.

THE MYSTIC MARRIAGE OF LUCASTA.

O NIGHT of fragrance, on these open downs—
On these unlimited, exalted downs —
Descend, descend !   I yearn once more for thee !
Thou art more precious still, more beautiful :
Thou penetratest more and more the deep
And hidden fount of visionary thought !
Thou art so cool, so vague, so mystical,
So close enfolding !   I adore the sea,
But I am passionate and mad for thee,
And for the luminous splendour of thine eyes,
And thy moon-crown of burnish'd, burning gold.
Mine inner being in the ample folds
Of thy black, beautiful, and boundless limbs
Is drained in sensuous delirium ;
And in ecstatic, universal bliss
The soft luxuriance of thine unseen mouth
Draws all my spiritual strength away
In frenzied, fascinated utterance.

O occidental light of saffron gold,
Collect thy dilatory splendours now,
And linger not !   With all thy dews and stars
Enfold me, Night, in infinite embrace,
Let me lie with thee on these open downs,
A naked soul, with every inmost part
Responding, by a tingling sense intense
Of an immeasurable luxury,
To thine unstinted, unrestrain'd embrace.

So cried the spirit of the wandering scald ;
Night answered him— Night answer'd me, the scald—
And Night with Spirit in communion join'd
Had progeny of prophecy and song :
And then the visionary mystic rose,
With inspirations as with mantle clothed,
And wings endow'd, transcended starry Night,
And, with the chrism of a psychic love
Baptised, virginified, regenerate,
To saffron Morn's auroral-rose embrace,
To thee, Lucasta, came, thou morn of soul,
Thou mother-fountain of Time's kings to come,
The continent of lips, the clean of heart,
Creation's human crown.   As earthly night
By stellar steps to blessed day leads on,
So mystic Night, Lucasta, leads to thee,
And thou, mine Eos, to a Golden Age

Which every scald foreshew'd, but one fulfils—
Strike, harps of Angels! harps of God, the Scald!
Strike, harps of Kings! Strike! Io EVOHE!
With choral chants proclaim the Golden Age

When in a solemn solitude apart
I watch for visions amid God's mystery
Of dying sunset and of tender sky,
And smell dry fragrance of the thirsty hedge,
Which supplicates the tardy evening dew,
While busy sparrows on the ivied elm
Chirp out their secrets all unconsciously,
And I interpret by a magic art
Not vainly learn'd, the ferret from the dells
Bounds frighten'd by, the burnish'd beetle halts
To let me pass, the blackbird hops before,
And some new interest of floral life,
Of beasts', or birds', distracts in joyful way
From over contemplation, step by step,
The dreamer's mind. These influences soft
Of sylvan things confer receptive moods,
And some new image for thy shining crown
Of memorable emblems Nature grants,
Or some new name, which happy fancy wins,
Thou child of " Nature's bridal ecstacy,"
Who in the nuptial night of heaven and earth
Wast procreated on the pyschic plane,

And somewhat thinly clothed with starry flesh—
By spirit interpenetrated oft—
Art now commission'd into worlds of sense,
With magic, life-illuminating words
Of everlasting love, celestial pledge,
Delivering.   Indelibly this day
Those holy words are written in my heart,
And when for us the bridal morning comes
A Mystic Marriage shall be made therein,
A crowning and consummate spectacle,
Where I shall wed with ideality,
Where I shall wed with thee, mid pyschic pomp,
Poetic pageantry.   The sunset land
Shall lend its banners, and the night her stars,
The morn her dew-spread garlands. Then shall rise
A choric grandeur from the infinite sea,
The grand, immeasurable, endless sea,
The holy, holy sea.   Light from the full,
The smiling earth, light from the moon and sun,
Light from the mind of man, the soul within,
The deathless spirit overbrooding both,
Light out of fancy lands, from elfin shores,
Light from imagination's loftier realms,
Light from the desolate, the awful wastes
Of magic worlds involved by woful spells—
Light concentrated, light ineffable,
Light shall be round us then, shall clothe us then ;

The splendour bursts e'en now, O sky of grey,
Which veils insufferable sunset gold !
O lonely lanes and vistas in the wood,
Which twilight fills with mystery !   Wan star,
White star, first star, pure font of trembling light !
O deep, adorable, ecstatic hush,
Which fills my soul with longings for the far,
The unattainable, the sky-bound verge,
Profounder hush and higher mystery !

By application of the alchemy
Of purged imagination, fix'd intent,
I will diaphanise mine outward self—
A process possible but hard attain'd,
One of the sciences of faeric land—
And then by aid of well-directed will's
Unlimited ability, I'll drape
Thy virgin body for a bridal robe
In living light.   On nuptial couch of dream,
Star-dighted, in a house of prophecy,
And overbrooded by a moonlit vault
Of visionary violet, star-sprent,
With a most perfect spiritual embrace
I'll compass all thy being.   By an art
Man masters only on immortal heights
Out-pinnacling Parnassus—magic heights—
The astralising of my soul and flesh

Shall be so perfect, eminent, complete,
Accomplish'd with such plenitude, that by
The secret contact of that bridal night,
Thou shalt thyself transfigure to the mind,
And thine eyes' ravishment, thy heart, thy limbs,
Shall kindle all the potencies of soul—
Stars in thine eyes and moon upon thy brow,
Morn's saffron in the masses of thy hair—
Shalt thou pass off through dreams to Deity.

The Interlude.

A ROVER'S HYMN.

ONCE I wish'd a thousand things,
　　Thoughts that soar on eagle wings
Follow'd in their soaring;
Now my raptures rarely rise
Further than thy dear grey eyes,
　　There mine ardours pouring.

Oft in midnights lone and still
Fancy fleeted far at will
　　Through the starry spaces;
Now it dreams, both day and night,
Round about one only light,
　　Shining where thy grace is.

O for darksome forest haunts,
And—for him no danger daunts,—
　　Wilds and wildernesses!
Open seas to sail far over,
Dizzy peaks, to draw the rover,
　　Draped in gleaming dresses!

O to dare both height and deep,
Where the Kraken lies asleep,
 Where the last star quivers,
Where the last word of existence
Through the darkness, and the distance,
 Life to void delivers !

And beyond all space and time,
Far transcending speech or rhyme,
 Out of thought's dimension,
That one central point to win
Which all secrets centre in,
 By a soul-ascension.

May God's mercy grant me these—
Nature's "primal sanities,"
 And high Truth's unfolding !
In such dreams my life exhaled,
Till thy tender form unveil'd
 Unto my beholding.

Then the light of rose and gold
Gather'd up from vale and wold,
 From the sky descended,
Shifted off the open sea,
Came and draped thy symmetry
 In a garment splendid.

All the beauty named in truth
In thy tender human youth
    Visibly inhering,
Breaks the ancient spells investing
Speculation's fields of questing,
    At its first appearing.

Melody of merle in copse,
Mavis in the poplar tops,
    Lark at morning's gateway—
How thy laughter's silver lightness
Robs the bird-world of its brightness,
    And absorbs it straightway !

Now the sunset lights may kindle,
And the mild moon wax and dwindle,
    And the winds keep calling,
While the Alpine hills point o'er me,
While the long paths wind before me,
    Falling, rising, falling.

And the bright, the lucent distance
Open realms of new existence,
    Keen and cold and splendid ;
See the spirit in its trances
There uplifted, there advances,
    Lone and unattended !

Unattended, lone, untiring,
Upward, onward, still aspiring,
　　Through the light and glory—
O the grandeur ;　Ah, the breathless
Heights and flights unfolding, deathless
　　Voyager, before thee !

But the distance gleams in vain—
To immeasurable main,
　　Grand in tidal diction,
To sidereal expansions,
And to scintillant star-mansions,
　　God give benediction !

When the furthest flights are ended,
And the furthest heights ascended,
　　The last star transcended,
All the world's resource expended,
Be the roving soul commended
　　Unto love more splendid—

Love more splendid still than all,
May its blessings him befall,
　　Inner worlds disclosing !
O may space's final verge
Into Christ's own light emerge,
　　There be his reposing !

But for me the dream is o'er ;
Through the outer world no more
 Roving and exploring ;
Past the beauty of one face
Do I look to greet Christ's grace,
 In love daily soaring.

Has the rover lost or gain'd ? '
Has the thinker, tax'd and strain'd,
 Balancing and proving,
Lost the vista, lost the vision,
Sinking all the sense of mission
 In the sense of loving ?

Nay, thou art an open sea,
And a green world fair and free
 Meet for love's emprising ;
In the depths of thy grey eyes
Brood a thousand mysteries
 Souls may sink or rise in.

So, with mystic love my guide
In thy woman-nature's wide,
 Magian world I enter ;
There the tranced thinker wanders
Ever there the rover ponders
 Voyaging and venture.

The Fifth Parable.

THE REGENERATION OF LUCASTA.

IS that thy voice which deep in haunted glades
   Expounds the passion of the nightingale?
Is that thy smile beneath whose fruitful glance
The wheatfields mellow on these Kentish cliffs?
Is that thine eyes' light on the gleaming sea?
Is that the dainty fragrance of thy breath
In hyacinthine dingles deeply sunk,
Possess'd by spells and odours? Is it thou
Whose beauty's light, in amaranthine blue
And glory draped, looks down on joyful earth,
And royal majesty of open sea,
From such unmeasured distance? Hast thou won
Thy dimpled whiteness from the sea-gull's wings—
Thy splendour drawn from heaven's blue ecstacy—
Thy freedom's grace from fountains—from the depths
Of brooding ocean thine unsearchable
Profundity of spirit-speaking eyes?
Or dost thou lend thy nature's boundless wealth
To beautify the Cosmos?

The ravish'd spirit into trance ascends—
Again—again.   I reach the world of mind,
I reach that world where all things dream'd may be,
If by sublimity and beauty they
Can urge a claim on life.   Uplifted there,
By night and day, and glimpsing still beyond,
And soaring still, and winding far away,
The spiral stairs of being, which transcend
The uttermost infinity, my soul—
Impassion'd by the poetry of love—
Beats now with eager wings through starry space,
Aflame with inspiration, seeking out
That process hidden in the psychic plane
Whereby the beauty of a mortal maid
May with the luxury and wealth of light—
The radiant, adorable, supreme,
The highest good, desired of all our eyes—
Be visibly emblazon'd. . . . . I have found
The secret path, I know the perfect way,
By which the streams of spiritual life
Flow down to vivify the minds of men ;
I know the channels of receptive mind
Can open out and more that flow receive,
Till, every bank o'erflow'd and floodgate burst,
Through all the pores and particles of flesh
It radiates and coruscates and glows
In visible splendour bright—to purge, to cleanse,

To clarify, regenerate, baptize,
And with electric shock to wake in man
Affinities with Godhead, as the sun,
With gentle heat on tender days in spring
Fills germs with teeming life, makes buds unfold,
And all the inner power of new-born things
Evokes to outward beauty and delight.

The secret path is found, the perfect way ;
And when, Lucasta, far from human life,
I set thee down, after an arrowy flight,
Beside the lone coast's utter solitude,
And fill thy spirit with the ocean's voice,
As lone sea caves are filled ; shall haunt thy brain
With singing winds and clamour of joyful birds
In heaven afloat ; thine eyes of trust and love
Transfigure with an ardent violet
From the bright zenith's royal altitude ;
When sunset's light of rose has tinged thy cheeks,
When lanes and gardens full of floral scents
Have made thy breath magnolian ; when thy speech
To day-long melody of summer months
Is modulated ; when harp-harmonies
Have mellow'd the movements of thy limbs ;
When I have set thee with thy hair unbound
To meet the magic of a moon at full,
And by an adoration of the soul

Pour'd out to Dian, the beloved, the crown'd,
The plenteous queen, have drawn a virtue out
From her benignant beams of tawny light
To glorify thy tresses ; when the stars
Have overwatch'd thee ; when the saintly night
Has tranquillised the waters of thy soul ;
When thou art hush'd, and hallow'd, and subdued,
And vitalised, exalted, and made strong ;
And when the veils of matter and of time
Are rent and torn, and when, beyond their shows,
The scald-magician to the secret truth,
The secret beauty points, and that within
The fair illusion of thine outward form
Makes answer, leaping towards the actual
With parabolic bursts of melody—
Then from the glory of a thousand stars,
With lifted hands, I'll draw the secret light
To pour on thee, to pour on soul and mind,
To make a visible splendour in thy flesh ;
And thy first nuptial dream of Deity
Shall pass into a consciousness divine ;
And sanctified, regenerated, high
Uplifted, an illuminated soul,
The Mystic Marriage of that bridal night
Shall be completed then, Lucasta shine
To light the age when every maid and boy
Shall equal glories wear, her crown assume,

Where, in the earthly city of the blest,
No sun shall set, nor moon shall need to rise,
But there the Christ-light of the human soul
In house and street abide.

The Interlude.

THE BENEDICTION OF LUCASTA.

ONE dainty, soft, and fruitful shower of rain
    Has purged and clarified the fragrant air,
On this God-favour'd evening, late in spring.
It shines as lucent as thy virgin brow,
Lucasta mine: to every slightest stir,
Its cool, translucent particles, replete
With a most sensitive, subtle, soul-like life,
By tremulous emotions far prolong'd.
Respond in chiming cadence—the lark's song—
The seething murmurs of the shifting sea,
Plunged in the pleasaunce of a mood of dreams—
 The temper'd merriment and melody
Which in the church bell sounds, recalling oft
The benediction of thy beautiful voice,
Which lifts my soul into Eternity.

Then falls a gleam upon the open sea,
Which is not blue nor grey ; the placid, pure
Perfection of thine all-delighting eyes—

Thine eyes' true light—shines magically there.
God bless the wonder of those waters deep !
God bless thine eyes, whose beauty fills my life !
God bless that lark whose frenzy haunts the sky !
God bless thy voice, whose modulated tones
Have spell'd full often many a waste of waves,
And oft Astarte bound through formless nights,
When tempests raved, to pour her soothing light
On riven landscapes in the inner world !
God bless the ripples of thy laughter, all
My nature lifting to love's mantic height,
The inspiration which is poesy,
And bold ambition towards all noble deeds,
All spiritual flights of life and thought !
God bless thee ever, and in all thy ways !
I stand this night upon a lofty down ;
A dreaming city by a dreaming sea
Beneath me spreads, bewitch'd in dreaming air ;
Round me are solitude and wilderness.
With all the potence of immortal will,
I called God's rain of benediction down
To water all the paradise of thy soul.
Descend, Celestial and Deific Dew !
Rise Eden Incense, and thy virtue sweet
Diffuse around thee, as the clover fills
These fields uplifted with its teeming scent !

The Sixth Parable.

THE DIVINE MISSION OF LUCASTA.

THE silent pageantry of sunset draws
    The exiled dreamer forth down winding roads,
Where bindweeds close their vein'd and trailing cups
About the treasure of the first cool drops
Of evening dew. Thou, also, wayside rose,
Thy fragile petals delicate of tint,
And permeated with felicitous
But unobtrusive fragrance, dost uplift
Thine airy chalice. May a gentle rain
Refresh thy buds; may ever thorns protect
Thine elfin beauties from the rustic hand;
May temper'd winds about thine arbours green
Breathe light in modulated melodies;
May golden bees when thy full bloom is come
Thy mellow sweets extract to fill their hives
And honeycombs; with wings of azure gauze
The moth which haunts the fruitful fields beyond
Above thee hover; may thy heaven ne'er want
A lark to sing in; may thy fabled love,

The nightingale, through all night's holy space
Of vision and of mystery abide
In glow-worm lighted thickets close at hand,
And all the senses of thy floral soul
With rapture ravish ! . . . Have I bless'd thee well ?
Lo, now thy blush is in the western sky !
Above the orange, o'er the azure blue,
It slowly steals.   A solitary star
With solemn expectation high uplifts
The astronomic spirit, which is vow'd
To adoration under starry heights
And furthest flights of spiritual thought.

All day I've tarried in the burning fields,
Awaiting Night.   The sun has tann'd my skin,
The heat has sapp'd my strength, a parching thirst
Consumes me.   Minister in cooling dew,
In gentle rain, in vivifying wind,
And in the shelter of thy plumage soft,
And in the refuge of thy bridal breast,
Receive and hide me now, supernal Queen !
Bid all thy plaintive nightingales begin
In vale and thicket !   Droop thy pinions down,
And quench that burst of occidental light
Which through thy sea-born panoply of clouds
Has torn so suddenly. . . . The splendour fades—
Where art thou now ?   Stoop, beautiful and grand

Unbind thy tresses, let them fall on me,
Diffuse thine odours round !   With thy bright eyes,
Thy beautiful, innumerable eyes,
While I adore thee, gaze !   Now thrill me through
With mystic whispers in the wind and trees—
How wonderful, how mystical thou art,
How deep thy secrets are !   Thy tenderness
Surpasses all, and I am lost in thee !
Thy cool, unconscious kisses on my mouth
Are pattering in aromatic rain ;
Lean over, press me, breathe into my mouth,
I read thine eyes like poems !   Speak to me—
Speak ever to the spirit that hast form'd,
And consecrated with Uranian love,
And astral chrism of a scald elect.
O Night of odours and of sanctity !

And lo, the darkness, like a loving mouth,
Parts in the utterance of a bell-sweet name ;
The stars stand closer round, the trees incline,
From every quarter of the open world
The mystic name LUCASTA softly breathes ;
A fragrance foreign to the land and sea
That trisyllabic harmony distils. . . .
May the strong influence of naked heaths,
Of aromatic odours brought from far,
Of voices speaking from the heart of things,

Of inspiration and divinity,
Of Night's unutterable loveliness
And boundless breadth of being, concentrate
And pour on her !   O may her gentle form
Become a porcelain vessel for the night's
Ecstatic myrrh and essences of nard !

The utter rapture seems a moment's space,
But all the starry hours elapse therein ;
And stars recede, and aureate morning gleams,
Its marvel fills the zenith ; the black wings
Are lifted from me, there Lucasta shines ;
The darkness blossoms into open day—
Do thou, Lucasta, bloom, the Day of Christ.
With potent seed of spiritual song
'Tis mine to fill thy virgin womb of mind,
Which out of poetry conceiving light,
Shall with a glorified intelligence
Illuminate the new humanity,
Shall people the regenerated earth
With hierarchies of heroes and of gods,
Who in a dual stream of perfect life
Shall issue from thee and shall flood the worlds.
I see them crown'd with vital beauty's bright
And coruscated splendours—maid and youth
Join'd in one magic band of chastity—
A biune spirit, with a cosmic blaze

Of planetary glory circling round
A solar marvel of wind-woven hair
In spiral aureole.   With gleaming limbs,
Whose loyal loins of continence contain
The ecstacy, the ravishment, the joys
Of generative Nature : with full breasts
Of honey'd milk, with mouths of melody,
With earnest eyes of everlasting love,
They stand, the innocent, the illuminate,
The youthhood and the royalty to come—
Thy sons, thy daughters reign--celestial fruit
And magnum opus of consummate bliss,
When in thy gentle nature's inmost shrine
The Bridal Spirit unto Mystic Love
Made modest ministry.

The Interlude.

A Vision.

I KNOW some dreadful, most exalted doom
   My future waits.   My soul is taken hence
And set full often by a stormy sea—
A grey, perturb'd, immeasurable sea—
The desolation of whose terrible voice
Transfixes all my being.   There are clouds
Heap'd by the wild art of a winter wind
In wild confusion.   There is saffron light
Through lurid rifts.   The verge is tooth'd by waves,
The whole sky torn by tempest.   There are sharp
And bulging headlands, promontories bleak,
And melancholy miles of winding coast,
With stones and seaweed strewn.   No sea-mew cries;
I stand, wind-wrapp'd, and   dream   deep   dreams
      thereby,
Or wander aimless, waiting, hush'd and white,
Some fierce convulsion in the boding sky.
My soul is shrivell'd by the fire of thought.
My frame is search'd and pierced by icy winds

Mine eyes are fixed upon the raving waste
Of whirling waves, and, utterly apart
From every sympathy and voice of man,
I face with madden'd faculties alone
The mysteries of being.

                  I accept
The doom.   My spirit has been tortured there
But has not fail'd.   An inspiration comes
From misery, from desolation strength,
From Nature in convulsed, terrific moods
The solemn secret of supernal things.
I hail that terrible and rending scene
A threshold of revealment.   That rent sky
Will open suddenly, in depths serene
A sunset all of majesty and light
Revealing ; clouds transfigured grouping round
Will lead imagination on from world
To world of thoughts ineffable.   Some ray
Will fall full redly on the restless sea
And soothe its tortured surges, smoothing out
A path of magical and mystic light—
Salt breeze and rosy splendour—all whose length
My soul, uplifted in a mighty trance,
With faculties made clean, with tranquil step,
Will swiftly traverse. . . . To the Land of Light
Go, favour'd Soul !   A magnet draws thee on :
The spiritual prospects open wide,

Dream preludes vision ; like a flower of flame
Unfolds high vision into truth attain'd ;
Thy pinions bear thee to ecstatic rest,
In quiet seas of spiritual space
Profoundly lapp'd. . . . The magnet draws thee on ;
Thou art awaken'd in the world of mind,
Whose hosts of beautiful and perfect life
Are gleaming round thee, poised and sphered at length
Upon the heights of supersensual things.
An emblematic but objective world
Prolongs its shining vistas far and wide,
And ministers in beauty and delight
To thy refined perceptions. Life therein
Takes form according to the loftiest laws
Which rule thine own imaginings purest types
And fairest images of truths all thought.
All dream transcending. Thou art taught thereby,
Thou art inspired; the end of all is seen—
How man proceeds through death to birth anew
In more refined and more significant worlds
Of typical phenomena; in each
Is taught, prepared, and led to face at length
The naked and unutterable truth
Whose essence is the Deity reveal'd.

And when the vision into night recedes,
The soul descends, and in some wondrous way

I stand and look into Lucasta's eyes,
The whole significance of outward things
Unrolls before me, as a scroll unwinds,
And in the hyaline and crystal depths
Of her unspotted spirit do I read
Infinities of meaning.

The Seventh Parable.

The Transfiguration of Lucasta.

THE summer storm has ravaged wide and far,
　　The rent sea, madden'd, flings its tortured crests
In savage tatters to a writhing sky,
Defiant of the lightning.　All the air
Is rack'd by winds; the firm, establish'd earth
Itself makes answer to the thunder's shock
With spasms of portentous shivering.
Reverberation and vibration both
Combine about my path to terrify;
But, like a necromantic Magus wall'd
And fortified by mystic circle, poised
Erect and central there, with pointed sword
And prominent pentagram, commanding thence
Chaotic crowds of elemental souls,
Which headlong surge against that mighty line,
And break like billows into formless spume—
The dregs and lees of life—adoring love
Of Nature, manifest in milder moods,

Doth now protect me like a four-fold shield;
And as the fishes when a tempest tears
The surface of their glorious element,
Plunge down to still, immeasurable depths,
I sink unconscious to consummate calm
In dream-world's oceanic bowers profound.
When from this mystic matrix of the mind
The virile spirit into time returns—
" Lo, I make all things new !" creative Light
Cries sparkling forth from every globe of rain;
With rose-leaf softness falls the tender night,
Its breath—the moderate, mellifluous air—
With aromatic odours softly blent
In delicate proportions, intertwines
Among the unbound meshes of thy hair,
And in the alabaster "entrance gates
Of melody," with low-toned breathings soft
And infinitely modulated, makes
A silken rustling.   The bindweed twines
The sincosity of spiral sprays,
With graceful terminals of pendant bells—
A simple chaplet—round thy dainty head,
And drooping down in errant elegance
About thy shoulders falls in gladsome gleam,
And slowly folds—Lucasta—into sleep.

O luminiferous and azurine,

Immeasurable vault of holy sky,
Thy living purple soften slowly down
Through hyacinthus and through heliotrope
To opal's pallid and evasive charm!
And in the twilight let Lucasta's eyes,
Dilating gently, as a soul expands
Within the vital light of noble thought,
Ineffably diffuse a conscious light
Of holy, human love! Descending dew,
The long-desired, distil thy purest drops,
These scattered tresses cool and consecrate!
My nature softens in a pool of love,
Which is the Mystic Water of the Wise,
Apollo's Baths, removing all things rank,
All imperfections, superfluities,
Which pass in fumes and leave the Mystic Stone,
The Perfect White—ineffable, supreme,
Inclusive Love, which flows for all mankind—
My dove of Dian, my Hesperian Tree,
My Phœbus bright, my oriental Pearl,
My Psychal Chemistry which tinges life
And aureates the Cosmos.
                                    Nature drinks
The sacred, deifying soma draught
Of dews and moonlight; then in every leaf,
In each light breath which stirs its magic sleep,
Vaticinates about us, pouring forth

An aromatic blessing, which, in turn,
Exalts my spirit, as its pulses beat
By thee, Lucasta, as a virtue falls
In broad vibrations from the trembling beams
Of that orb'd moon aureoline, whose eyes,
Whose lucent eyes are turned alone on thee :
While by thy being's mediation sweet,
And through thy luminiferous nature's love,
As through the vistas of a magic glass,
The world transfigures, . . . Thou art Isis now,
The manifested mother of the Gods.
An unimaginable splendour fills
My spirit with an infinite prophecy,
And in the floral future of the world
I stand translated, in that golden age
The royal line begotten of thy pure,
Elected body, has by psychic art,
After the pattern in the poet's mind,
Created.　On the summits of the soul
The four-square city of the Salem new
Stands high erected, stands the House of God,
The final Temple of Humanity.
This is the bright and everlasting day—
The Lord hath made, this is the Day of Christ;
And thou—the mystical and moonlit morn
Which did that day of majesty forerun
And by conception did originate—

Art in beatifying memory
And venerating love that lifts thee up—
A joy transfigured through the infinite—
Held in the endless age.

                              I lose thee now ;
Thy glory passes on its grand ascent,
Beyond the narrow range of mental sight,
Along the circle of Eternity.
I stand in vision on the timeless plane—
What part for me in the divine romance,
Ye stars of prophecy, is granted there?
Lucasta shines this eve a simple maid ;
I wake the splendid and titanic dream
Of Psycho-solar majesty by strong
Ecstatic force of penetrating will
In all her being.   May its end achieved
Find one star-chaplet for the poet's brow
Whose medial mortality received
The inspiration from seraphic heights,
And permeates the spirit of his bride
With magic ideality

Epilogue.

YE scornful crowds, far hence—far hence, profane!
    There falls a rapture on my heart and mind
Above the measure of all sordid thoughts,
Above the common reach of intellect,
Above imaginations based on clay.
My lips are cleansed with spirit-kindled flame,
My features shine, mine eyes are glorified
With a strange, mystical, and purple light,
And I am beautiful a little space.
O golden light which swathes both mead and hill,
Beatifying sunset, flood the world!
Shew open downs, illimitable sky
Incarnadine, and brood on maple leaves,
On oaks and orchards brood!   O little space
To shine with borrow'd beauty, lengthen out!
O sweet new sense of happiness and health!
O ever to be beautiful and free!
Thou sacred charm, thou presence in the eyes,
Thou grace of inmost deity ungauged

Which from the furthest vistas of the soul
Uplightest outer life--abide awhile ! . . .
The day is spent, alas ! the glory fades,
The borrow'd glory from thy beauty caught,
When by a privilege and grace supreme
Of magical election, I was set,
By dread imagination's awful aid,
To utterly transmute thy mortal life
With supermortal beauty, and behold
The ravish'd wonder, the uplighted shrine,
The soul, the soul unveil'd.

                That deed is done—
That wonder compass'd—*consummatum est*—
And thou art bound to me by holy ties,
By intimate and infinitely close,
Indissoluble, spiritual bonds
Of magic's strong affinity.   Thine own
Imperishable part, thy human form,
Its every phase of mien, thy lineaments'
Innumerable changes, every light
And transitory gleam of gentle thought
Which beautifies the planets of thine eyes,
Are wholly and irrevocably mine.
O Love, the moon above the vanish'd sea,
Above those silent waters merged in mist,
Uplifts the splendour of her perfect disc
With hay-time halo ring'd, and fills the sky

With golden glamour. . . . Turn thine eyes on me!
Consummate altitudes of azure sky's
Immeasurable distance fill my soul
With boundless exultation.   When I seek
Some lofty ridge which fronts the boreal fount
And source of souls, and evening's balmy wind
Breaks tide-like round me, bathing all my frame
With viewless billows, fragrant, cool, and fresh,
And life-infusing, then some psychic force
Expands my faculties, the length and breadth.
The beauty, the resources of the world
I realise.   And when with patient, fond,
Discerning eyes, I gaze and gaze on thee,
Thy nature's possibilities unfold,
Thine own inherent joy, thy light, thy might ;
Elected mother of the life to come,
Of unborn nations, kings and priests to be,
The holy hierarchs of intelligence.
I see the new regenerated earth
With emanant humanities divine
From thy most sacred, pure, and fruitful womb—
The matrix of the cosmic man to come—
As with resplendent blossoms, all adorn'd
In everlasting May-time of the mind.

By God's auroral redness far diffused ;
By that bright, beautiful, supernal hope,

Which makes an eminent lustre in my soul;
By all associations of romance
Which bind me close with unobtrusive ties
To simple things—white roads and winding lanes,
And country inns, and certain upland slopes
Which moons transfigure, or to ancient lore,
To tales of prowess in the times of old,
To truthful chronicles of knightly deeds
And kingly quests and faërie ventures wild ;—
By mine own spiritual enterprise,
My pilgrim travels into mystic realms,
My psychic explorations far prolong'd,
My progress there. the triumphs still to come,
The prophecies, the presages, the signs
Inscribed upon the spiritual sky,
And timeless wonders stored Beyond the Gates;
By most of all the iron force of will.
Which fells and fills and levels and makes smooth,
Which crushes opposition ; O by all
Unfolding prospects, as I speak reveal'd,
Height over height, of infinite romance,
With golden dreams emblazon'd— I am pledged
To perfect thee.   My soul is staked thereon,
All crowns thereon contingent.   I have search'd
Thy nature's depths with sp'ritual eyes,
And all its possibilities reveal'd
Have bound beyond revoke through life and death

My whole devotion, my resources all,
To compass their development.
                              Receive
These canticles and parables, wherein
Thy soul's creation in prophetic thought
Is dimly sketch'd! The mountains round 'r   l
Heights beckon, blue, illimitable vault,
Pierced by the snow-capp'd peaks, exalts and thrills.
I take thee hence, I lead, I lead thee on;
The aspiration, the desire, the will
Uplift us both; thou art no more of earth—
The troubled ocean of created things
Remotely gleams and glimmers. O the wings
Which bear thee now—the Morning Dawn which
        breaks
And floods thy stars with everlasting light,
Auriferous, intolerable light
Of circumambient sunshine! . . . . It is Love,
Strong Love proclaims these heights, this path reveals,
Which lifts thee up, which will not, will not fail!
The Faërie World, the mystic Avalon,
Sword-guarded Eden, and those gardens bright,
Those shadow palaces, those haunted mosques—
Irém, the wandering City, are in thee
The permanent possession of my soul,
O Garden Rose, O Lily of the Blest,
Pomegranate of the Paradise of God,

My cistus white, syringa pure and sweet,
My glory-marvel of Magnolia!

Now, God be praised Who made thy gentle soul,
And Christ the Word by Whom thy soul was made,
And those beneficent, wonder-working gods
Who shaped the plastic matter of thy frame,
And soften'd all the geometric curves,
Contourine symmetry for matchless limbs,
For grace of poised head and holy breast,
Eliciting! Be bright Aurora blest,
Who under sacramental veils abides
Within thy nature's virgin sanctuary!
Bless'd all the stars that shape thy future ways!
Bless'd all who love thee and are loved by thee!
Be thy true lover in thy beauty blest,
His dreams ideal, taking shape in thee,
And truth ecstatic, truth triumphant, truth
Illuminant, the deathless Crown of Life,
Attain'd in thee. The Daughter of the Voice—
Bath-Kôl the Mystic, Daughter of the Voice—
Makes answer in the Infinite—Amen!

Miscellaneous Poems.

Azalea.

ONE dream is over now; the morning dawns.
    The beautiful and visionary night,
Moon-haunted all its length, by winds inform'd.
Star-litten plenitude of pure romance
And inspiration, temple of high thought,
And mystic, consecrated house of love,
The worshipful and spiritual night,
Has in this grey and disillusion'd morn
Been slowly merged. The coarse and common life
Begins to stir. I wake, I stand alone—
One billow broke upon the sea far out
This moment pass'd ; it flash'd a seething crest,
Then fell. No space for inspiration now,
No magic left, no message in the sea!
The once bright-shining moon is bleak and white
And burnt to cinders. When the trees were draped
In solemn darkness, in their mien was awe,
Their aspect majesty, their rustling leaves
Dodonian prophecy—they were mighty thoughts

Made typically visible, not trees.
The spell is broken; as a part once more
Of vegetable nature, they stand stripp'd
Of poetry and meaning. The lark's song
Is just the singing of the morning lark;
The engine's drawn out, melancholy shriek
Fills all its silver pauses far prolong'd,
And drowns with dismal wail its golden close.

O bitterness! There is no human word
To give expression to the infinite depth
Of desolation in a human heart;
The futile methods of our mortal speech
Choke sympathy by commonizing grief.
Thou art gone, gone—O misery! I learnt
Such spells to beautify thy house of life,
Now am I as an alchemist bereft
Of sophic sulphur and of mercury.
I made by magic in a winter month
A Paradisal garden full of bloom—
The holy lotus in its lakes abode
With plumaged swans, and all its paths were lined
With lustrous lilies. The azalea fill'd
The consecrated air with grateful light
From myriad blooms. Thou hadst no care therein;
I spent the strength of spirit on thy dreams—
To crowd the magic hush of maiden sleep

With pleasing idealities.   I search'd
The world of mind to deck thy maiden bed,
In amaranthine bowers, with purple blooms
Of dim inviolable violets
Whose scented heads received thy psychal limbs
And soften'd moss beneath. . . .   The morning broke—
Then was a latch upon the garden gate
Uplifted by thy voluntary hand
And out from poesy, from purple light
Of high, adorable, divine romance,
From ecstacy of dream, from magic hush,
Into the commonplace, material world
Thou didst go forth.   A poet's arms embraced thee,
A poet's lips have dwelt and dream'd on thine,
A poet's eyes, by conscious act and art,
With magic skill thy beauty's mortal grace,
And passing charm transfiguring, had clothed
With utter immortality, but thou
Hast chosen earth.   I had been god for thee.
I am a priest, I swear, a mission'd man—
High Nature, delegate of God supreme,
Imposed pontifical and holy hands
Upon her prostrate postulant, ordain'd,
Commission'd, consecrated, set apart,
And dedicated to her ministry
And sacred service, me deserving not,—
Me miserable lifted, royal robes

Of inspiration made my soul assume,
And set me ever at her secret shrine
To sacrifice.
      The blush of Morning bursts
Above the dim and wavering line of downs
And sends a sanguine glory up the sky,
Whose lofty and immeasurable arch
Transforms from grey to lavender, and fills
With sudden ecstacy of morning birds . . . .
The charm arrested leaves thee clay once more.
I might have leaven'd thee with angelhood--
Attest it, Prophecy, imperial Dreams,
A thousand Songs attest . . . . And thou art gone !
Thou art not wholly false nor wholly true,
Thou art not clay nor spirit, and the world,
God knows, may leaven thee—one golden chance
Thy foolish heart rejecting, leaves thy life
Bereft of glamour and divinity.
But lo, the dream remains to comfort me !
For me, the mortal part alone hath pass'd.
I have not lost ; 'tis thou hast fallen short
Of immortality and beatitude,
Because I would have clothed thee with a love
Of power unparallel'd.   I pictured thee
In mystic samite, zoned and lily-crown'd,
Even so would I have crown'd thee in thy mind ;
God's secrets fashion'd into shining stars

Had shone upon thy forehead as a light
To lead humanity, to lead the world,
Torchlike, to truth and Him ! There was no height
Beyond the will-ability of soul
To scale for thee. There was no height beyond
The heights to which my spirit would itself
Have lifted thee. O poised in purest space,
Seraphic, sunlike, crown'd, beatified,
Intolerable God-light seething round
Thy beauty's blaze, beyond all time and thought
My poet's art ineffable, intense,
Had set thy soul infallibly—and now,
My God, and now ! . . . I see thee deck'd with
        pearls
And turquoise rings, and splendours brought from
        East
And West invest thy body. Thou art clothed
With earthly wealth instead of phantasy.
O sole and only truths of deathless mind.
O intellectual realities,
O infinite, intolerable lapse
From starry heaven of seraphic mind,
Of sacred, inmost, pure, unclouded mind,
The everlasting, the adorable,
To the gross, coarse, and commonizing wealth
Of earthly riches ! Can I wish thee bless'd
In these, or mated unto mortal man

Ascribe thee true beatitude therein ?
Thou wast a spirit in my arms' embrace,
And I transfigured in thine own became
A god beside thee, deified thereby.
How art thou fallen, O Lucifera !
But ecstacy of passion never quench'd
Exalts me ever up the heights of soul.
O upward ever !   O the endless height !
Which meets the bottomless abysmal depth
In the infinite circle of Eternity.
Light for thee still—O somewhere, somewhere Ligh
O further charm !   O strength for steeper path !
If I eclipse thee in my angelhood,
O thou too pure e'er to be wholly false,
I'll clothe thee in the mantle of my light,
And on my shoulders raise thee past myself
To heights beyond me !

In Aridity.

THE road is brown, a hundred yards below
   It dives full steeply—aspen, elm, and ash,
With graceful willow, at the sides thereof
Make shade and music round it.   It has rain'd
Through all the morn, but now the August sun
Is warm and brilliant, flooding mead and down—
Far hills are flooded, tiles of gabled farms
And distant churches glow. . . . . I gaze on all
The manifested beauties of the world,
And have not lost the vivid sense of charm
Which all can weave. The power of speech is mine,
The strength of love—why seems the tide of song
Arrested in me?   Thou inspiring God,
By bard and prophet commonly invoked,
One in thy varied names, I call on Thee—
Forsake me not!   Abide in song with me!
The grace of inspiration still vouchsafe!
I am a poet: I can see, below
This constant flux of outward surfaces,
One soul in all ; and in ecstatic trance

I stand by hedges where the fern and oak
With modest hawthorn interweave and blend
The variations of their greenery,
And there the gnat which buzzes in the air
A busy message of continual life—
Of life in all, of life through all and all—
The cool fresh wind which stirs in flower and frond,
In leaf and twig, in every blade of grass ;
Which tempers summer at its thirsting noon,
Awake some random thought to bless my life,
As dews bless eve.   Descend once more on me —
Descend ; I call thee in the name of all
Which soothes and vivifies—thou fire of God !
Thou "light that never wast on land or sea,"
Transform the world !   Thou inner sense of sight,
Transform my soul !
     The fountain seal'd awhile
Is broken now, the speech from heaven descends—
From yon intolerable, azure sky,
Which hath no cloud to stain its virgin depths,
It *does* descend—and AVE, AVE, EARTH !
The Poet cries; the Priest of Nature puts
His vestments on, the prophet's mantle wears,
And offers praise again.   A thousand trees
Take up the message; may the winds prolong—
The distant hills re-echo—all is song !

A Sea Prophecy.

AN infinite shimmer on the open sea—
    A thousand, thousand lights ! To cross thee
  now,
And ever—ever—ever—sail away,
Till with thy vastness, with the mighty vault
Which rounds thine urgent being, I am one—
One with the stellar ministers of night
Who populate the spaces of the air
Above thy breezy bosom, one with her
Whose path of pure, illuminating light,
Through all the four-fold phases of her reign,
Is night by night, with blanch'd, transfigured face,
Perform'd in silent ecstacy—with these
To unify existence ! . . . I am yours,
Stars, Sea, Moon— Mother of all mystic thought !
Wrap me, ye Winds, away to some wild place,
Where, in the centre of a surging world
Of crested billows full of stormy speech,
My sea-dream bark is bound, awaiting me.

There is an ecstacy which passes speech,
There is an inspiration which transcends
Expression, there is joy which deifies;
The limitations of our mortal life
Dissolve therein; through every sense enlarged
The floods of rapture pour into the soul.
All these in generous measure have been mine,
But something waits me far from every coast,
From every harbour far—alone, alone !
The promise, the prevision cannot fail,
But drifting—drifting—drifting—night and day,
And drifting—drifting—drifting—moon by moon,
Amid revolving galaxies above,
The scenic splendours and illuminant glare
Of lissome lightnings, and the organ tones
Of rending thunder, over open seas
Of majesty and turbulence and might,
I shall go forth invincible, erect,
Inspired, to seek the threshold of my doom,
Whereon the crests and surges and sea-winds,
And all the echoing voices of the sea,
With one precipitous, infinite music crash,
Shall break and merge in revelating light,
In vistas, in low melodies, in speech—
In silver speech divine—of Spirit Land.

Stella.

THE mystic singer to a certain " Star "
    In salutation ! . . . Be thy secret name
Inscribed upon the Palace of the King,
And on the white apocalyptic stone
Indelibly engraved ! I paced at night
The City's streets; an inspiration came,
And, like a tempest, suddenly it rent
Through all my being. To thyself it bore
A mighty message, until now retain'd,
That from the sacred heart of sylvan things,
From woods and forests, from eternal downs,
From water-sides, the Golden Word might come . . .
In the mellifluous, melodious names
Of multitudinous angels, of divine
And ministrant immortals, and of high,
Supreme, exalted, everlasting kings,
The Golden Word descends to sun thy soul--
A formal promise of the Crown of Life
Assured in poem which is prophecy.

It bids me first recall thy nature's depths,
And next its heights, and then those sacred arts

With whose exalted themes thy nature holds
Impassion'd correspondence.   These are proofs,
And that outreaching towards ennobled thought,
That consciousness of purpose unfulfill'd,
Of thwarted mission, of exalted fate,
Whose plans miscarried, which I read in thee,
Are unmistakable, convincing proofs
That nothing is beyond thee.   In thy hands
Thy future lies; conceive what height thou wilt,
And, on the honour of the angel bands,
Thou shalt attain it, thou shalt reign therefrom !

My soul is set upon an endless quest
To span the bounds of being; on the heights,
The high-exalted, spiritual hills,
Towards which my face is set, behold, I swear
To greet thy spirit, be it late or soon !
Forth to the Light ! Forth to the height of God !
The tocsin call comes from the Infinite ;
All Nature taking voice, her organ tones
Have culminated in a single cry
Of clamorous accordance, urging on !
Speed on !   The arrow to the Star ascends,
Through mortal channel comes immortal speech. . . .

The mystic singer to a certain " Star "
His salutation sends.

BY THE SAME AUTHOR.

Bound in peacock blue, with an æsthetic and symbolic design. Price 5s.

A Soul's Comedy:

THE SPIRITUAL HISTORY OF JASPER CARTWRIGHT.

SOME OPINIONS OF THE PRESS.

" In this work Mr. Waite has produced a poem very much above the average of poetic merit. Though *A Soul's Comedy* is never likely to become a popular book, yet it will be read by many with a considerable amount of pleasure. Jasper Cartwright's struggle against the circumstances which have combined to ruin his spiritual existence, and his final triumph over them, are powerfully portrayed, and cannot fail to interest such as are thoughtfully inclined. . . . His blank verse is pleasing and melodious. Scattered at intervals throughout his volume there are passages of more than ordinary beauty."—*The Spectator.*

" *A Soul's Comedy* is a very extraordinary composition. . . . The story of this poem is in some respects very repulsive, and yet told with great delicacy and beauty.

Part of the book is the baldest prose, cut up into lengths ; part is unintelligible mysticism about magical studies ; and part—by far the largest part—is real poetry. . . . Its sustained poetry will well repay the reader, if he will put up with the bald prose of Mister Gilp, the school-master . . . , and the mystic nonsense of the magical part. . . . One merit should be noticed in encourage-ment of those who might be repelled by the opening of the story, viz., that it steadily increases in interest and in beauty until near the end. . . . Some songs or poems introduced into the narrative are very good ; one, a passionate address to a dead boy-friend, Gabriel, being especially beautiful. If the poem were recast in the sense that we have indicated, we venture to think that it would be entitled to a high place among the poems of the day."—*The Guardian.*

" Mr. Waite is possessed of genuine inspiration that lifts his work above the mass of wares sent forth every year to the world as poetry. The presence of an over-subtle mysticism, and even of an occasional tinge of Rosicrucian darkness, will not prevent lovers of poetry from enjoying the many passages in his play as re-markable for power of thought as for beauty of expression. Mr. Waite's sympathy with Nature and his descriptive powers are likewise of a high order."—*Literary World.*

" Some time has elapsed since we paid a sincere tribute to the beauty of *Israfel,* and we are not sorry to meet with another work from the same pen in *A Soul's Comedy.* . . . It may suffice to say in general that the poem, cast in a quasi-dramatic form, is a very noble one, though painful to a degree. The main idea of Jasper's origin is so horrible in its pathetic tragedy as to rouse reminiscences of Ford's masterpiece, and the after-episode of Mary Blake is little less distressing ; but out of these seemingly unpromising materials Mr. Waite has evoked a tale of human sorrow, struggle, and final triumph such as must appeal to the heart of every true man. . . . The poetry rises at times to unusual heights, as, for instance, in the description of Mary's death, the Benediction in the monastery chapel, Austin Blake's prologue to the third part, or, best of all, the scene where Jasper resigns Gertrude to his friend. . . . Jasper's prose fairy-tale is delightful, though not, it may be, suited to all comprehensions. . . . Taken altogether, this is a true and worthy poem."—*The Graphic.*

BY THE SAME AUTHOR.

Crown 8vo, parchment, red top.   Price 3s. 6d.

𝔌𝔰𝔯𝔞𝔣𝔢𝔩 :

LETTERS, VISIONS, AND POEMS.

Mystical Allegory of the New Age and the New Regenerated Humanity.

OPINIONS OF THE PRESS.

" If, as seems most likely, a small but appreciative audience will satisfy the author, the favourable reception of *Israfel:* letters, visions, and poems, by Arthur Edward Waite, need not be matter of conjecture ; the book must be both admired and prized by the few elect spirits fitted to appreciate and understand it.   For our own part, we should rank it very near to that marvellous work, *The Broadstone of Honour*.   It is undoubtedly true that the whole is pitched in far too high a key for the generality of modern readers ; some may be deterred from perusal by the subtle mysticism of much of the contents, while others, it may be feared, will fail to grasp the pure and lofty Christian ideal embodied in the letters and visions, but we may unhesitatingly aver that no man reading the work with a properly prepared intellect, and with a sympathetic mind, can rise from it without feeling better and stronger for the task. This is not the place, even did space permit, to enter into a discussion of the author's theme, but if any seek the keynote of the whole, we would refer him to the last lines of that fine poem, *The Higher Life*, or to pages 23, 24, and 108. The poetry is of a high order, and, apart from its more spiritual aspects, remarkable for a passionate appreciation of natural beauty, and for pictorial treatment. The blank verse is specially good, reminding one, perhaps, more of Cowper at his best than of any other poet, but thoroughly original both in style and matter. *Israfel* is one of those rare books which are part of the salt of the earth, but it is not for all readers."--*The Graphic.*

" To those who delight in magic and 'dabble in Babylonian numbers,' *Israfel*, by Arthur Edward Waite, will afford much comfort and consolation. . . . By way of a guess, we hazard the suggestion that *Israfel* is the ideal soul of man, distinct from individual souls, and personified in order at once to mirror and to magnify the aspirations of individual souls not yet at one with the universal. . . . The verse is harmonious, and not without a peculiar and original beauty."—*Westminster Review.*

" It is a long time since Horace said that poets have the right *quid libet audendi*, and the maxim seems to be acted upon to-day with no less confidence than it was, we may presume, when the Roman critic wrote. No flight appears to be too daring for the modern poet, and if his wild career leads him into the misty obscurity of the clouds, he will generally find a band of admirers to declare that it is the reader's obtuseness alone which prevents a due understanding of the poet's ideas. It may be that there are some who will grasp the true meaning of Mr. Waite's remarkable poem, *Israfel*, though we confess to a lurking suspicion that the author was animated by no very lively anxiety to make himself understood, even granting that he knew what he meant himself. . . . But we have the satisfaction of reading, among a great deal that is rather unintelligible, passages which bear the unmistakable stamp of true poetic talent. . . . We have quoted enough to show that Mr. Waite's poetry is of no mean order, and, after all, *Israfel* is a work of considerable power, and in parts quite intelligible."—*Literary World.*

" It may, perhaps, be gathered that the writer has, or has had, a friend of an exceptionally pure, exalted, and powerful nature : that in contemplating his character under an emotion similar to that which gave rise to the Laureate's *In Memoriam*, the writer, by employing the Divine exaggeration of analogy, has constructed to himself a conception of the nature of the angel or presiding masculine influence—its Michael, so to speak, of the new age or order, which in all spiritual aspirational natures is being now earnestly looked for, and, by some such, realised to be in actual operation. In realising the Divine personage symbolised, the symbolical human person is lost by, or absorbed to, the seer, who sees only the being symbolised, and celebrates in a distinctly deep and genuinely earnest spirit the virtues and Divine attributes of the angel under the name of *Israfel*. This inductive method of arriving at a spiritual conception by means of a material symbol, belongs, no doubt, to the higher order of mysticism. . . . Speaking generally, we should say that the profit of this book to most readers will not be its dogma, or body, but the spirit in which it is written. It is pure, elevated, and aspirational, and is, moreover, singularly free from that arrogant individualism which disfigures so frequently the utterances of those entering the spiritual region of life, and as yet unaware of the phantasies of the *Dwellers on the Threshold*. . . . The miscellaneous verse in the volume is very graceful."—*Light.*

www.ingramcontent.com/pod-product-compliance
Lightning Source LLC
Chambersburg PA
CBHW022148020726
47496CB00008B/2608